EASY
YOU

Young, Ed.

My Mei Mei.

$16.99

In fond memory of "Mom," Antonia Soriano Tuosto,
the embodiment of motherly love,

and

to Antonia and Ananda and all children who give their caregivers the opportunity
to stretch beyond their limits.

My Mei Mei

ED YOUNG

Philomel Books

I AM NAMED ANTONIA after Nonna, my grandma Antonia. When I was half, I joined Mommy and Baba in China. We flew home together.

As I grew older, I played *Jieh-Jieh*, big sister, with Mommy by blowing her nose.

And I played Jieh-Jieh with Baba
by changing his diapers.

I had a pretend *Mei Mei*, younger sister, called Jiang Hai, whom no one else could see. When we played, she always let me have my way. She even stood in for me when I got into trouble.

I once asked Mommy if I could have a real Mei Mei. Mommy said she didn't know how she could manage two. I brought two of my children to show her.

"Like this!" I said.

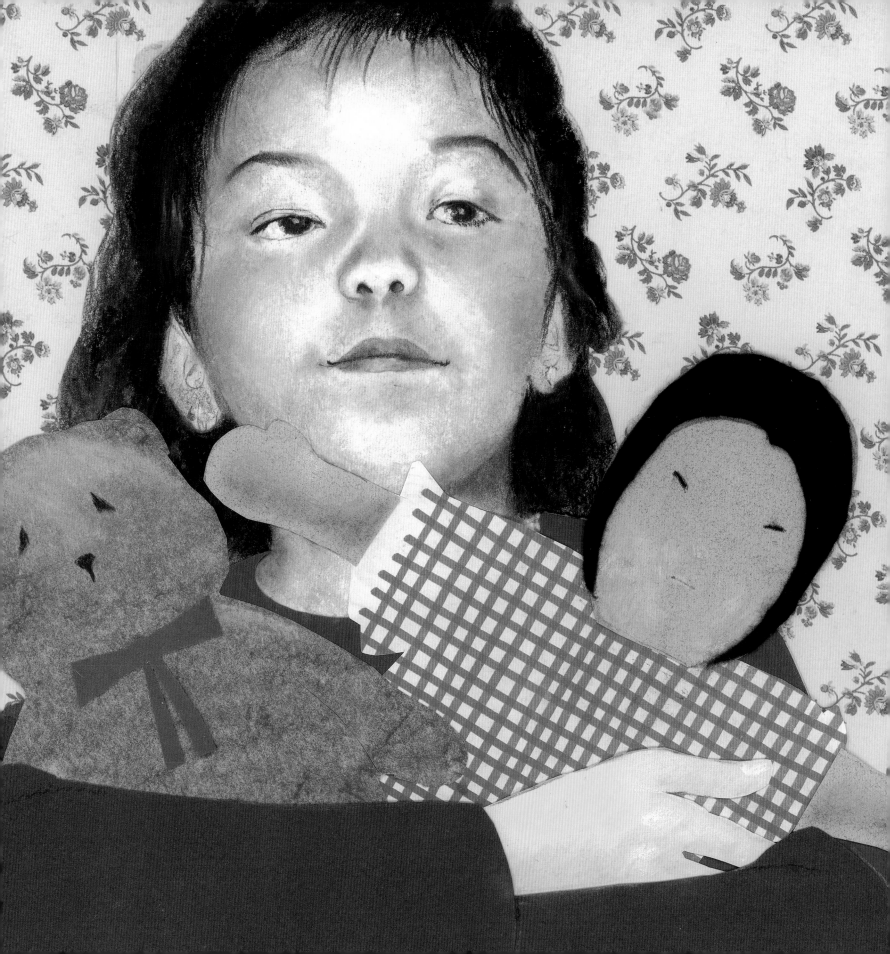

When I was three, we took the friendly sky to China to bring a real Mei Mei home.

In the dorm of a medical college, it was hot and wet. I was really excited; I drew pictures of our Mei Mei while we waited.

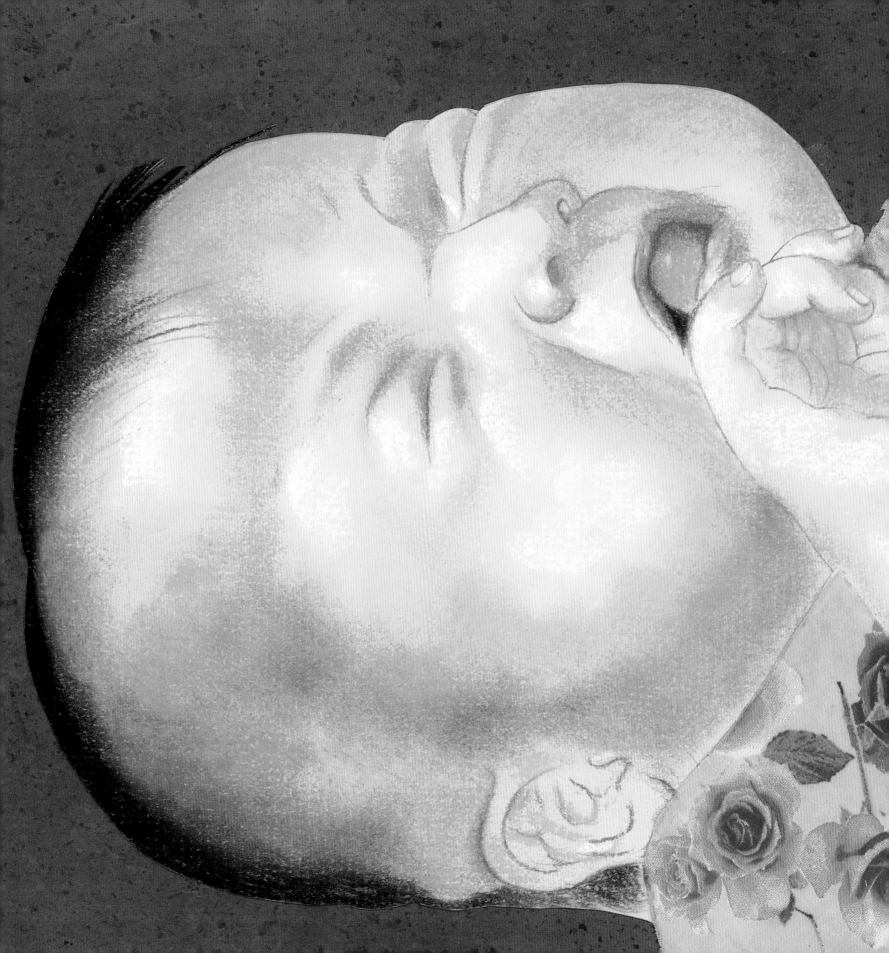

Finally Mei Mei was brought to us. She was scared, upset, and began to cry.

I offered her my Rachel to calm her down.

When we returned, I found out
that she was not what she ought to be.
She couldn't walk.
She couldn't talk.
She couldn't play.
She took all the attention away
from me.

I felt left out.

In time a teacher came to show her how to crawl and walk. Another teacher showed her how to talk.

One day she was given treats by her teacher. She asked for one more for me, her Jieh-Jieh. She wasn't bad all the time.

Soon after, a boy took her shovel
in a sandbox. I went and told him,
"She's my sister and I am bigger
than you!" It felt good to stand by
Mei Mei.

As she grew, Mei Mei came to see me off to school and to meet me after school. She made me feel big, as in my class I was small.

That summer we went to Cape Cod. On the beach at low tide I decided to take Mei Mei out for a walk. I told Mom, "No grown-ups allowed!" I showed her jellyfish and other dangerous creatures. We had fun!

We used to play Mommy and Baby
Cat. Now we have real cats.

We used to watch musicals and
nature films. Now we perform music
and mimic wild animals.

I help her with reading and math
so we can play more board games.

One day we went to Mommy and Baba asking, "Can we have another Mei Mei?"

Ananda and Antonia in Soochow, China, 2004.

I began thinking about this book ten years ago, on my daughter Antonia's adoption from China. Originally it was to consist of three separate paths that would merge in the middle. The first path: that of my wife Filomena's and my journey to get this child. The second path, a highly speculative one on our part: her birth mother's separation from her baby. The third, also speculative: the infant's loneliness and uncertainty as she was passed from one caregiver to the next in the first six months of her life.

As I was struggling to find a design where I could weave these elements into my book, a completely different story (A Pup Just for Me) came into my hands. It gave me the opportunity to deal with an adoption theme, but it was when we brought our second baby, Ananda, back from China that the story that I knew I wanted to tell fell in place. Not only was it a story about adoption, but about a sibling relationship. While creating this book, I was also struck by how quickly children grow. Literally, no sooner had I put words and pictures on paper, than both children had already outgrown them.

So, although the book is concluded, our story continues.

Ed Young

Patricia Lee Gauch, Editor

PHILOMEL BOOKS
A division of Penguin Young Readers Group.   Published by The Penguin Group.
Penguin Group (USA) Inc., 375 Hudson Street, New York, NY 10014, U.S.A.
Penguin Group (Canada), 90 Eglinton Avenue East, Suite 700, Toronto, Ontario, Canada M4P 2Y3 (a division of Pearson Penguin Canada Inc.)
Penguin Books Ltd, 80 Strand, London WC2R 0RL, England.
Penguin Ireland, 25 St. Stephen's Green, Dublin 2, Ireland (a division of Penguin Books Ltd.)
Penguin Group (Australia), 250 Camberwell Road, Camberwell, Victoria 3124, Australia (a division of Pearson Australia Group Pty Ltd).
Penguin Books India Pvt Ltd, 11 Community Centre, Panchsheel Park, New Delhi - 110 017, India.
Penguin Group (NZ), Cnr Airborne and Rosedale Roads, Albany, Auckland 1310, New Zealand (a division of Pearson New Zealand Ltd).
Penguin Books (South Africa) (Pty) Ltd, 24 Sturdee Avenue, Rosebank, Johannesburg 2196, South Africa.
Penguin Books Ltd, Registered Offices: 80 Strand, London WC2R 0RL, England.

Design by Semadar Megged.   Text set in 18-point Fournier.   Illustrations are rendered in gouache, pastel, and collage.
Title lettering by Ed Young based on Antonia Young's handwriting.

Library of Congress Cataloging-in-Publication Data
Young, Ed.
My Mei Mei / Ed Young.   p. cm.
Summary: Antonia gets her wish when her parents return to China to bring home a Mei Mei, or younger sister, for her.
[1. Adoption—Fiction. 2. Intercountry adoption—Fiction. 3. Sisters—Fiction. 4. Chinese Americans—Fiction. 5. China—Fiction.] I. Title.
PZ7.Y855My 2006   [E]—dc22   2005008097
ISBN 0-399-24339-9
1 3 5 7 9 10 8 6 4 2
First Impression